PARTY HEROES

Based on the episode "PJ Robot Takes Control"

This book is based on the TV series PJ MASKS © Frog Box /
Entertainment One UK Limited/ Walt Disney EMEA Productions Limited 2014;
Les Pyjamasques by Romuald © (2007) Gallimard Jeunnesse. All Rights Reserved.
This book/publication © Entertainment One UK Limited 2020.

SIMON SPOTLIGHT
An imprint of Simon & Schuster Children's Publishing Division
New York London Toronto Sydney New Delhi
1230 Avenue of the Americas, New York, New York 10020
This Simon Spotlight paperback edition August 2020
Adapted by Ximena Hastings from the series PJ Masks.
For information about special discounts for bulk purchases, please contact Simon & Schuster Special Sales at 1-866-506-1949 or business@simonandschuster.com.
Manufactured in the United States of America 0720 LAK
2 4 6 8 10 9 7 5 3 1
ISBN 978-1-5344-7108-5 • ISBN 978-1-5344-7109-2 (eBook)

Connor, Amaya, and Greg are walking to school. They are worried about Romeo's Flybots. Romeo invented those mischief-making robots to help him take over the world!

"Look!" says Greg, pointing at zap marks on the ground. "Romeo's Flybots are still out there."

The PJ Masks head to HQ and find PJ Robot at the Picture Player.

"Are you playing a game, PJ Robot?" Catboy asks.

PJ Robot shakes his head and points at the screen.

The PJ Masks take a closer look. It's Romeo's Flying Factory!

"It looks like those blue dots are Flybots," Gekko says.

"And PJ Robot is controlling them!" Amaya adds.

PJ Robot nods.

PJ Robot shows the PJ Masks that he can control the Flybots. He figured out how to connect to them, and now he can make them do anything . . . even dance!

"This is so smart, PJ Robot! We could take over the Flying Factory and stop Romeo forever!" Catboy says.

Back at the Flying Factory, Romeo is confused. He doesn't know why his Flybots aren't listening to his commands!

"What are you going to do now that you can control the Flybots, PJ Robot?" Gekko asks. PJ Robot shows the PJ Masks a party invitation on the Picture Player.

"A Robot party?" Owlette asks. "If all the Flybots just play party games, that will keep Romeo from causing trouble!"

"It will turn the Flying Factory into a Fun Factory!" Catboy says.

Suddenly, the Flybots start to change color. Uh-oh! Something isn't right!

"We need to go to the Flying Factory to save the day!" Catboy says. "We have to keep this robot party going!"

PJ Robot stays behind at HQ. He's a little scared of the Flybots.

The PJ Masks land at the Flying Factory.
"PJ Pests! I knew you were up to something!" shouts Romeo.
"Oh no," Romeo cries suddenly.
The Flybots grab him and force him to play a party game!

Then they trap the PJ Masks in their Flybot games!
Owlette is stuck spinning around and around.
Gekko is forced to play Pin the Tail on the Robot.
Catboy manages to leap out of the way and calls to
PJ Robot for help.

"PJ Robot, your remote control isn't controlling the Flybots anymore. Someone needs to stop this robot party!" shouts Catboy.

Even though PJ Robot is scared of the Flybots, he knows he has to save his friends.

When PJ Robot arrives at the Flying Factory, he zooms straight to the control desk!

"Be careful, PJ Robot!" Owlette calls.

PJ Robot has an idea. He connects to the control desk and then . . . the lights go off!

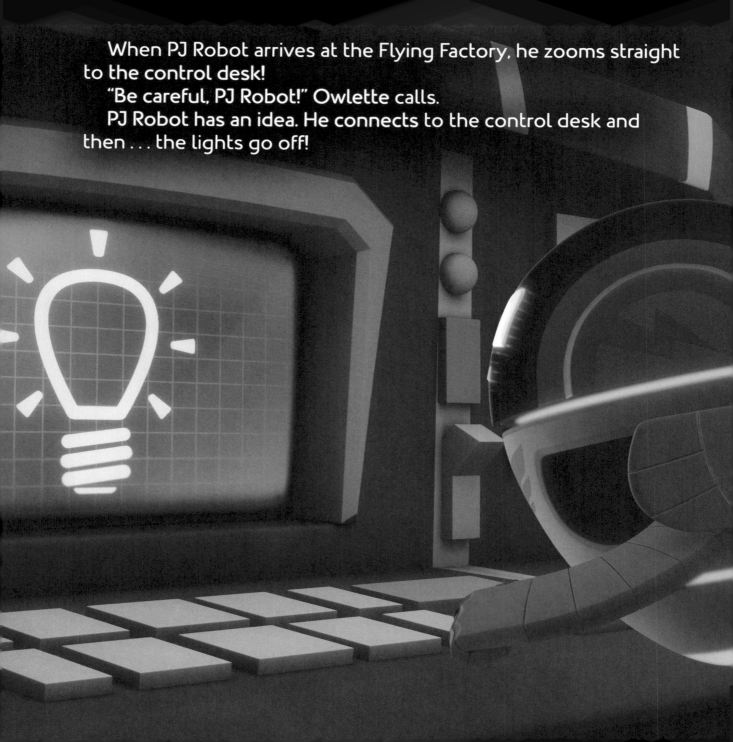

"PJ Robot? Are you okay?" Gekko asks in the dark.
Suddenly, a single spotlight beams down on PJ Robot.
He starts doing party tricks for the Flybots!
The robot party is back on!

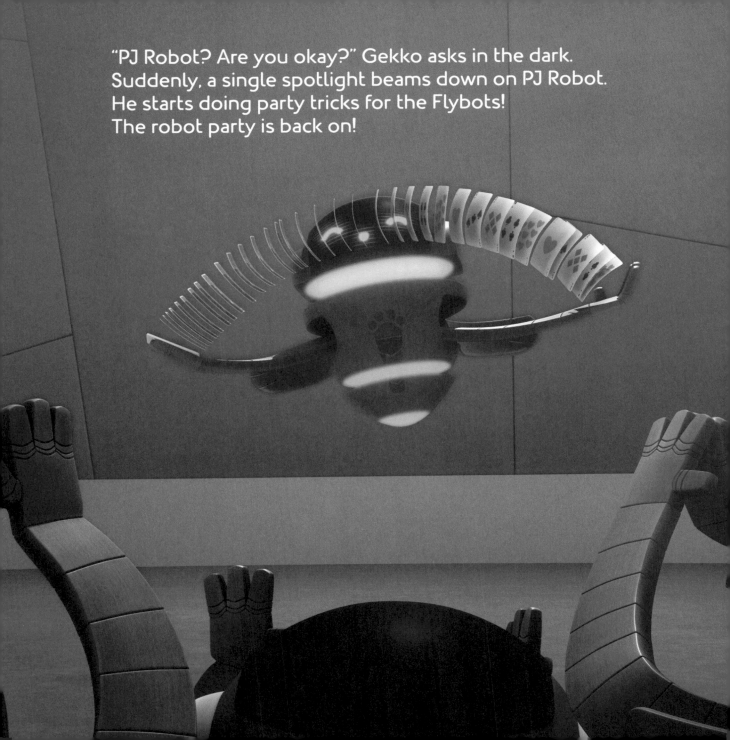

The PJ Masks are amazed.

"It's working!" Owlette says. "PJ Robot isn't *controlling* the Flybots, but they're not *out* of control anymore."

"I guess they like whatever PJ Robot likes . . . and he likes to party!" Gekko says.

The Flybots start cheering and dancing with PJ Robot.

"You call yourselves heroes?"
Romeo shouts. "I still need rescuing!"
The PJ Masks work together to
rescue Romeo.

Then everyone gets into the robot party spirit!
The Flybots start to sing:

"Master didn't take over the world,
Master isn't number one.
But we're okay, we're just fine,
'Cause we're having party fun!"

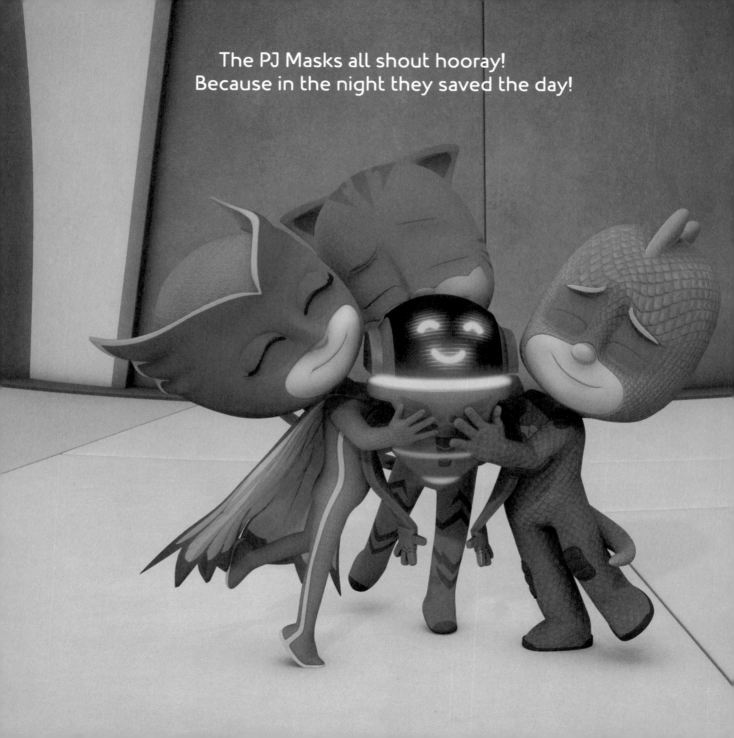

The PJ Masks all shout hooray!
Because in the night they saved the day!

Let's play Pin the Tail on the Flybot with the PJ Masks and PJ Robot!

Ask an adult to help you punch out the Flybot and tape it to a wall. Then, close your eyes and tape a tail onto the Flybot!

Ask an adult to help punch out the robot tails below!